This book belongs to

....

....

A catalogue record for this book is available from the British Library
Published by Ladybird Books Ltd.
A Penguin Company
80 Strand, London, WC2R 0RL, England
Penguin Books Australia Ltd, 250 Camberwell Road,
Camberwell, Victoria 3124, Australia
New York, Canada, India, New Zealand, South Africa

001 - 10 9 8 7 6 5 4 3 2 1

© Eric Hill, 2004
This edition published 2011
Eric Hill has asserted his moral rights under the
Copyright, Designs and Patents Act of 1988
All rights reserved
Planned and produced by Ventura Publishing Ltd
80 Strand, London WC2R 0RL

ISBN 978-0-72326-753-9

Printed in China

Time for Bed,
Spot

Eric Hill

It was getting late. Spot had finished his supper. Now he was busy playing with his train, his blocks and his ball.

Sally looked in.
"Time for bed, Spot," she said.
"But, Mum," said Spot,
"I'm not sleepy!"

"You can tidy up your toys,"
said Sally. "That will help to
make you sleepy."
"All right, Mum," said Spot.

He put away his train,
his blocks and his ball.

"I'm still not sleepy!" said Spot.

"A nice warm bath will help,"
said Sam, Spot's dad.

He filled the bath with lovely
warm bubbles for Spot.
Spot stayed in the bath for a long
time, playing with his boat
and his duck.

But, when it was time to come out, Spot still wasn't sleepy – not even when Sam wrapped him in a big, fluffy towel!

"I'll read you a story," said Sally.
"That will send you off to sleep."

Sally read Spot his favourite story. It was all about pirates and their adventures on the high seas.

"Read it again, please," said Spot, when she had finished.

So Sally read the story again.
"Thanks, Mum," said Spot.
"Maybe I can go to sleep now."

"Just close your eyes and
you'll soon drift into
dreamland," said Sally.

Spot closed his eyes and Sally kissed him goodnight. Then she tiptoed out of the room.

But Spot STILL wasn't sleepy!

"I can't stay in bed when I'm not sleepy," he said to himself. "I'll get up and pretend to be a pirate, like the ones in my storybook."

Spot went to his dressing-up cupboard. He got out an eye patch, a bandana and a wooden sword.

"Yo-ho-ho!" he said, jumping up and down. "I'm the pirate king of the high seas!"

After a while, Spot got tired
of being a pirate. But he still
wasn't sleepy!

"I'll pretend to be something
else now," he said, looking in
his dressing-up cupboard.
"What will I be?"

"I'll be a cowboy!" Spot decided.

He put on his cowboy hat and he found his horse. Spot rode his horse all around the room. Stomp! Stomp! Stomp!

"I'm a cowboy!" he shouted.
"This is so much fun – it's a good
thing I'm not sleepy!"

Sally came to the door.

"You're supposed to be asleep!"
she called. "What's all the
noise about?"

But Spot didn't answer.

That's because Spot didn't hear
her. He was curled up in his
dressing-up clothes – fast asleep!

Sally picked up Spot and tucked him into bed.

"I think I was sleepy after all, Mum," he murmured.

"I think you were," said Sally, smiling. She gave Spot a hug and another goodnight kiss. "Sweet dreams, Spot! Sleep tight!"